In the Woods

Robin Stevenson

orca soundings

ORCA BOOK PUBLISHERS

To my grandmother, Mormor, with love.

Library and Archives Canada Cataloguing in Publication

Stevenson, Robin, 1968-
In the woods / written by Robin Stevenson.
(Orca soundings)

ISBN 978-1-55469-201-9 (bound).--ISBN 978-1-55469-200-2 (pbk.)

I. Title. II. Series: Orca soundings
PS8637.T4871565 2009   JC813'.6   C2009-902578-7

First published in the United States, 2009
Library of Congress Control Number: 2009927571

Summary: When Cameron discovers a baby abandoned in the woods,
he tries to discover whether his sister is the mother.

MIX
Paper from
responsible sources
FSC
www.fsc.org   FSC® C016245

*Orca Book Publishers is dedicated to preserving the environment and has
printed this book on paper certified by the Forest Stewardship Council®.*

Orca Book Publishers gratefully acknowledges the support
for its publishing programs provided by the following agencies:
the Government of Canada through the Canada Book Fund and the
Canada Council for the Arts, and the Province of British Columbia
through the BC Arts Council and the Book Publishing Tax Credit.

Cover photography by Getty Images

ORCA BOOK PUBLISHERS
PO Box 5626, Stn. B
Victoria, BC Canada
V8R 6S4

ORCA BOOK PUBLISHERS
PO Box 468
Custer, WA USA
98240-0468

www.orcabook.com
Printed and bound in Canada.

14 13 12 11 • 5 4 3 2

Chapter One

I'm in the living room watching TV when the phone rings.

"Hello?" I am trying to sound casual in case it's this girl from school, Audrey, who I happen to have this huge crush on. And who just happened to ask for my phone number today. Only because she got stuck with me as a partner for a social studies project, but still…

"Cameron? It's Katie."

Not Audrey. My sister. My twin sister, though people generally find this hard to believe. "Mom's not home yet," I tell her, flopping down on the couch.

"I know. I just wanted to talk to you."

Me? Since when does Katie voluntarily talk to me? "Listen," I tell her, "I'm sort of expecting a call."

"Oh. Well, okay. Um…I guess I better let you go then."

I'm about to hang up, but something stops me. Something in her voice.

"Where are you?" I ask her. "Is everything okay?" I make a face to myself. In Katie's universe, something going wrong would mean getting an A-minus instead of an A. It would mean coming second at the swim meet instead of first. Katie is Miss Gifted and Talented. Miss Most Likely to Succeed.

Katie gives a weird, unfunny laugh. "I'm fine."

I sit up. "You don't sound very fine." There is a long silence, and I start to feel nervous. "Katie? Are you still there? What's going on?"

"I just…" I can hear her take a deep breath, almost a gasp. There's another silence. I'm about to say something when she clears her throat and says, sounding almost normal, "I need you to do something for me, okay?"

"What?"

"Um…you know that trail around the lake?"

"Sure." Some of the kids from school party out there, but I haven't been for ages. Not since last summer. Me and some of the guys from the football team went out there in August to drink beer and barbecue burgers and swim in the lake. "What about it?"

"Could you go there?"

"What? Now?" We used to go there for picnics when we were kids, with Mom and Brian the Pervert, but a trip down memory lane seems unlikely. We don't talk about that time period, ever. Also, Katie and I do not hang out together. Not that we don't like each other—we're just very different people.

"Yeah. Now."

"Why?"

There's a long silence, like it hadn't occurred to her that I might want a reason.

"Anyway," I tell her, "I can't. I don't have a car, remember?"

"Take Mom's."

I snort. "That'd go over well." I had a fender bender last year. It wasn't my fault—the other driver had slammed on his brakes right in front of me—but Mom muttered something about safe following distance, like that was even possible in rush-hour traffic. She told me her car was off-limits. It sucks. Of course, things like that never happen

4

to Katie. She is allowed to use Mom's car whenever she wants.

Not that she needs to anymore. Mom bought Katie her own car a couple of months ago. Me? I got a new bike.

"Cameron." She sounds impatient. "Please."

"Mom drove to work today, so I couldn't even if I wanted to. Which I don't. Anyway, what's the big deal? What's going on at the lake?"

"You could ride your bike," she says. "It's not that far."

I snort. It's a good half-hour ride, minimum, and that's pushing hard.

"Cameron?"

"Yeah." There's something freaky about this. Katie's not the type of girl who creates big dramas and mysteries about everything. She's usually ultra-sensible. Maybe she's had some kind of psychotic breakdown from too much studying. "Tell me why and I might consider it."

Or not. Audrey might call. She could be trying to call right this minute. I stand up and glance out the window. "It's starting to rain."

"It is?" Katie's voice breaks, and she sounds like she might start to cry. "Oh god…please? Cameron, I swear I'll never ask you to do anything again. Ever. Just do this one thing?"

I glance across the room and catch my reflection in the hallway mirror. I don't know why, but I am nodding to myself. Apparently some part of me has already decided to do this crazy thing for her. Whatever. I could use a workout anyway, and I have a brand-new mountain bike that I've barely ridden. "Okay, okay," I say. "I'll go."

"Don't tell anyone," she says.

Then she hangs up, and I wonder what exactly I have just agreed to.

Chapter Two

I scrawl a quick note for Mom—*Gone for a bike ride, back by 6 PM.* It's May and not that cold, but when you're cycling and the rain is coming down, you ge pretty chilled. I'm wearing an undershi and a light sweater under my cycli jacket, but I forgot to put gloves on. the time I hit the highway, my fing are practically frozen to the handleb

Damn Katie. I don't even know what I'm supposed to do when I get to the lake. Cycle around the trail and come home? I can't believe I agreed to do this.

The wind is blowing straight down the highway, against me. I duck my head and pedal faster. Story of my life: I always have the wind against me, and Katie always has it behind her. While she's pulling straight A's and applying to universities for fall, I'm still having trouble with just about every subject. Learning disability, the teachers and consultants and learning assistants call it. Screwed up, I call it.

A truck zips past me and sends a sheet of dirty water up in my direction. I flip the driver the bird. Damn Katie, I think again. My fingers ache with cold. I debate turning around and heading back home, but for some reason—stubbornness maybe, or curiosity—I don't do it. I take the turnoff toward the lake and think about the times we came here when we were kids. Fourth-graders. It was a year after Mom and Dad split up, and Mom was seeing Brian the Pervert. We didn't call him that then, of course. He was her first boyfriend after the divorce, and Mom said part of the reason she fell for him was that he was *just so great* with us kids. Ha bloody ha.

Not that he ever tried anything with me.

I pull into the empty parking lot and glide to a stop. Katie's car isn't here. I hunch my shoulders and wonder again exactly what she expects me to do now.

Even though Brian the Pervert has been out of our lives for years, I still think about him whenever I come to the lake or ride my bike by where he used to live. Even though I was just a kid at the time, I feel kind of guilty about not knowing what he was doing to Katie. Eventually she told some kid at school, who tol her mom, who called social services, and it all blew up. At first Mom didn't believe it. She didn't quite accuse Katie of lying and ruining her life, but that was how Katie took it. We all had to go for counseling, and Brian the Pervert left. Somehow it eventually blew over, and life went back to normal.

It's so strange that Katie would want me to come here. I don't think she's been back here since those picnic days. She's not the party type anyway. She has her friends, but she's not hugely social. The school swim team was her big thing, but she quit that back in January. Needed more time to study, she claimed. As if. Katie could pull off A's without ever cracking a textbook.

I wonder if Katie was here when she called me, and if so, why she took off. Nothing about this makes any sense, but since I've come all this way, I figure might as well ride the loop around the lake before I head back home. I cycle across the gravel of the parking lot and onto the packed reddish dirt trail. Tall trees stand green and slick-wet, branches dark against the gray sky, and the air smells like dirt and rain. Ahead I can see the lake, as flat and gray as the sky above. I slow down as I ride past the picnic area. It's a large grassy expanse with a muddy beach and half a dozen graffiti-scarred tables and a public washroom that's always locked.

At that party back in August, Audrey and I had this incredibly intense conversation at one of those tables, and I thought maybe something might happen between us. Nothing did though. I was too chicken to try anything. I didn't know if she'd be interested, and I didn't want to risk looking like an idiot. So we lay on this table looking at the stars and we talked for hours, about people and how we're all connected and the meaning of life and all that, and I totally felt like she got me in a way no one ever has. And then her friends yelled that they were leaving, and she left with them. When school started in September, we both acted like the whole conversation hadn't even happened.

Maybe when she sobered up she was just relieved that she didn't make the mistake of hooking up with me. I don't know. But by October she was going out with Dexter Harris, who is one of those supercool guys who is friends with everyone. Even I had to admit he was a good guy, despite that fact that he had crushed any hope that I might get together with Audrey. That was eight months ago, and as far as I know, they're still an item.

Audrey and I haven't really talked since that night at the lake. Even if she does call me, I know it will only be to work on our project...but a stupid part of me thinks that maybe if we spend some time together, she'll remember how well we connected that night. Pathetic and totally lame—that's me.

I cycle back into the woods and there is a sudden hush as the trees muffle the *splat-splat* sound of the rain on the lake and turn it into a soft whispering patter that is almost music. And then, over the rain-music—or through it, woven into it like one more part of the melody—I hear something else. A faint, faraway sound. It takes me a minute to realize what it is, because it is so out of place and there is no one around and it doesn't make sense. But as I listen, it gets louder and clearer, and there's no doubt.

It's the sound of crying.

Chapter Three

I get off my bike and lean it against a tree. Then I stand, silent, and try to figure out where the sound is coming from. I can't make sense of it. It's not loud—I can barely hear it—but somehow it sounds close. I step off the path into the ankle-deep mixture of dirt and decaying leaves and feel the dampness of it leeching any last traces of warmth from my frozen feet. "Hello?" I call out. My voice sounds hollow in the stillness of the woods. "Hello?" I say again, louder this time. I'm talking to myself, trying to make myself feel less creeped-out.

It doesn't work. I can still hear the crying.

I take another step into the woods. For a second I wonder if it could be Katie making that sound, hiding in the trees, waiting for me to get all freaked-out before she leaps out, laughing her head off. But I don't think so. Pranks aren't really Katie's thing. She's never been a big joker.

Maybe it's an injured animal. Do people set traps around here? Maybe a cougar, or…I don't know. A raccoon. Could a raccoon sound like that? So… human? There's a prickling feeling at the base of my spine and my stomach is twisting itself into one big knot.

"Don't be so stupid," I whisper to myself. "Get a grip." I take another step and a stick cracks loudly under my foot. I'm so tightly wound that I practically pee my pants. The crying has stopped, and all I can hear is the rain. *Damn Katie.* There's nothing here except me and my overactive imagination.

I'm about to head back to the path, back to my bike and out of here, when something catches my eye. A brightness, a color, something that doesn't belong in this place of muted greens and browns. A flash of blue. Something sticking out from behind a tree. I move toward it, around the tree, bend close. It's a bundle of blankets. I pull back the top layer cautiously, and there it is. Not a raccoon or a cougar or anything that belongs in the woods.

It's a baby.

A freaking *baby*.

It's tiny—newborn, I guess. Its eyes are closed and its face has blood on it, and for a minute I think it's dead. Then I remember the crying and I sort of push it, poke at its chest, just gently, and its eyes sort of flicker open for a second. I bend closer and I can see that it's breathing.

Holy shit.

Now what am I supposed to do?

I pick up the baby, blankets and all, and start yelling for help. I scream at the top of my lungs for a couple of minutes before I realize that there really is no one else here and that I have my cell phone in my pocket. I unzip my pocket, awkwardly, one-handed—I don't want to put the baby down, which is stupid, since obviously it's been lying here for a while, but it just doesn't feel right to put it on the dirt. Somehow I manage to dial emergency, and I'm waiting for the ring, waiting to say I'm at the lake and I've found a newborn and please send the goddamn ambulance like *right freaking now*, but instead my phone po up a little low-battery message and shuts itself off.

Crap.

I just stand there for a minute. I'm almost crying, to tell the truth, and I can't think what to do next. Then the baby gives a little grunting cry and I wonder how long it's been here. The parking lot isn't that far, but there was no one there, and it'd be at least a half-hour's walk back to the main road to flag down a car. What if that's too long? God, what if this kid dies while I'm carrying it? What if I show up at the main road with a dead baby? Walking isn't an option. But riding a bike while carrying a newborn is probably not considered terribly child-safe. On the other hand, nor is letting a baby freeze to death.

I lay the baby down in its blankets and strip off my jacket and my sweater. Then I pick up the baby-bundle and tuck it inside the sweater. I tie the bottom of the sweater in a knot so the baby can't fall out, and make a sort of sling, tying both sleeves together and slipping it over my head so that the baby is against my chest. Then I put on my jacket over top. It just zips shut, holding the baby snugly in place. I hope.

I get on my bike carefully. When I look down, I can just see the top of its head. Then I remember that we lose most heat from our heads, so I pull the sweater-sling over top. About two seconds later, I get scared that I'm suffocating it and I uncover its head again.

I don't have a clue what I'm doing. I've never even held a baby before. This is hardly the ideal first baby-holding experience.

"Don't you dare die," I tell it. "If you die, I'll be emotionally scarred for life. You don't want that, do you?"

The baby doesn't answer.

"I mean it," I say. I start pedaling as fast as I dare. "Look, I'm trying to help you. I'm gonna get you some help. Get you to a hospital, where it's warm and you'll get...I don't know. Milk. You'll get milk. You'll like it, honest, just hang on..." I am rambling. I can't help it, and there are tears running down my face. "I'm doing my best here, okay? Don't die, don't you dare die. I'm doing my best."

Just for once, I think, please please please, let my best be good enough.

Chapter Four

The trip out to the main road only takes a few minutes, but it feels like a lifetime. The baby seems to be breathing okay, but it's lips look kind of blue-gray. I can see it's heartbeat pulsing at the top of it's head, and I don't know if that's normal. I mean, shouldn't the skull cover the soft parts? It's a bit freaky, though it's also reassuring to see that he is obviously still alive.

I get off my bike and stand at the edge
of the road. There are no buildings or
anything, just empty fields on both sides
stretching all the way to the highway.
The first car I try to flag down just drives
on past, and I realize the driver probably
thought I was hitchhiking. The next car
slows to a stop, and I rush forward, heart
racing, but the woman behind the wheel
looks at me suspiciously and takes off.
I'm left standing there, yelling furiously
after her as the rain pours down. I have
never in my whole life felt so completely
helpless.

Maybe I should just pull the baby
out of my jacket and hold it up in front
of me.

There's a lull in the traffic, and no
one drives past for a minute. I wonder if
I should ride all the way to the highway,
but people might be even less likely to
stop there. There's nowhere to pull over.
yell a few swear words loudly and then

feel bad about the baby hearing them. Not that it can understand, but still, it seems sort of wrong that the first words this kid hears were those particular ones. "Sorry, little guy," I say. "I'm just a bit worried, you know? A bit stressed about getting some help for you. Just hang on there. Life is going to get better, it really is. If you just hold on, you'll get to do all kinds of cool stuff. You'll eat peaches and swim in the summertime, and you'll learn to ride a tricycle, and maybe someday you'll even kiss a girl. Not that I'd know anything about that myself."

And then a small car appears over the hill and slows down. The driver's a woman, and I think for a second that I probably look too crazed and desperate to be trusted, but she actually slows down, pulls to the curb and stops. I don't make the mistake of running over this time. Instead I unzip my jacket and point at the baby. "I found it in the woods," I say. "Can you call an ambulance?"

"What is…? Oh my god! A baby? You found it in the woods?"

I think for a second of Hansel and Gretel and the abandoned children of the fairy tales Mom used to read us. "Yes. By the lake. Can you please…?"

She gestures to the passenger seat. "Get in. It'll be faster."

I scramble into the car.

"Can I see the baby?" She looks at me. She's middle-aged, a big lady with graying dark hair and large tanned hands and a confident voice. "My name's Lainey. I'm a nurse."

"Um, I'm Cameron." I struggle to untie the sweater sling, then give up and just lift it over my head. The baby doesn't weigh anything. "He's still alive," I say stupidly.

She just nods and takes the baby. "Good."

"Um, I could sort of see his heart beating. In his head, like, on top there?" I point. "Is it meant to be like that?"

"Yup. That's normal. The skull isn't closed yet in a baby. Just a sec." She's counting, checking the baby's pulse and breathing. "Okay, hold the baby against you and keep it warm. Five minutes to the hospital."

She drives fast, but not crazy-fast, heading onto the highway. "The skull can't fuse before birth. It has to be able to give a little to fit through the birth canal."

Up until this moment, I hadn't thought about anything but this baby and getting it to the hospital. But that mention of the birth just made me realize that someone— some girl, some woman—gave birth to this baby and left it in the woods.

"I don't understand how someone could do this," I say at last. "Leave a baby out there like that."

"You don't know whose baby it is?"

"No. God. This is the…the sickest thing I've ever seen." I glance down at the baby's head. "He could have died."

"Mmm. Easily. How'd you find him?" Her eyes are on the road, hands steady on the wheel as she takes the exit to the hospital.

"I was just riding my bike and I heard a cry," I say. And then I think of Katie, sending me on her crazy errand. Was this just a freaky coincidence, or was this the reason she wanted me to go to the lake? How the hell could she have known about the baby? Helping someone hide a baby…I can't see it. I think about her two best friends and wonder about each of them in turn: Nikki, star of the swim team, freestyle record holder, off to Ottawa in the fall to study journalism. Luba, who coaches the junior swim team and works with disabled kids after school and still manages to pull off the same marks as

Katie. But neither of them was pregnant. There was no way. Even if they'd wanted to hide it, I don't see how they could have. I mean, they all see each other in their swimsuits practically every day.

And then my stomach drops as I remember: Katie quit the swim team four months ago.

"Sure you don't know who it could belong to?" Lainey asks again. Her voice is calm, almost casual, but there's nothing casual about the question.

I push the thought aside. It's crazy, anyway. Katie wasn't pregnant. I'd have known. She hasn't even had a boyfriend yet, nothing serious anyway. Besides, she's hardly the baby-dumping type. Katie's hyper-responsible.

I look at Lainey and shake my head. "I don't have a clue."

Chapter Five

The emergency room is busy, but Lainey doesn't bother to join the lineup at the reception desk. She just takes the baby from me and marches up to the counter. I hang back. The baby is passed to a short man in green scrubs, who disappears down the hallway. Mostly I'm relieved that someone else is taking over, but I'm not sure what to do now. I'd like to know that the baby is okay before I leave.

Then I realize that I just left my bike at the side of the road. My new bike. Shit. Odds of it still being there? About the same as the odds of finding a baby in the woods, I guess.

I glance at my watch. Six o'clock. Oops. I should call Mom.

Or maybe I should call Katie and ask her who the hell's baby this is.

I look around for Lainey and see her talking to a woman up by the counter. Then they both start walking toward me, and I realize that maybe all this isn't quite over yet.

"Cameron?" Lainey smiles, and I feel suddenly anxious. Which is stupid, because I haven't done anything wrong.

"Cameron, this is Nancy. She's the emergency room social worker."

Nancy holds out her hand, and I shake it awkwardly. I think of Nancy as an older person's name, but she's maybe thirty, tops, fair-skinned, with dark hair buzzed short on one side and hanging forward over her eyes on the other. Too many earrings to count, plus a piercing in one eyebrow and another in her nose.

"Can you come into my office to talk for a few minutes, Cameron? I need to ask a few questions, make sure we have all the information."

I shrug. "I guess. I should call my mom though. She'll be wondering where I am."

"Tell her you'll be a while," Nancy says. "The police are going to want a statement too."

"Um, police?" Maybe I won't call Mom right away. I follow Nancy down the hallway and into a small carpeted room.

She closes the door behind me. *Click*.

I haven't done anything wrong, I tell myself. So there's no reason to feel trapped. There's no reason to get freaked-out.

"They'll have to investigate," she says, sitting down. "They'll want to find the mother if possible."

I stay standing. There's a long silence. I think silences are some kind of counseling trick. I remember this from when we used to go as a family to see that therapist at the children's mental-health place. "I was just riding my bike," I say. "And I heard a noise. Crying." I shrug. "I guess Lainey told you the rest."

"Cameron, you brought the baby to hospital, which is great. You probably— well, almost certainly—saved her life."

"Her?" For some reason, I'd been assuming it was a boy.

"Yes. A girl." There's another silence, but this time I don't fill it.

Nancy leans to one side, one elbow on the arm of her chair, chin resting on her hand. Her fingernails are painted slick black. "If you are the father, you aren't going to get in trouble. Like I said, you brought the baby here and got her help right away. But…"

I just about choke. "No! Jesus. No, I'm not." It hadn't even occurred to me that anyone would think that. To be honest, even when I'd been trying to figure out who the mother could be, it hadn't crossed my mind that there was a father too. Duh.

"Are you sure? It'd be better to tell the truth up front."

"Christ. Yeah, I'm sure." Too goddamn sure, in fact. I've never got past second base with anyone, but Nancy doesn't need to know that.

"So it was just coincidence? You just happened to be there at the right time?"

I nod, mentally cursing Katie for getting me involved in this mess. Her words echo in my head. *Don't tell anyone.* I wonder what she knows, what she's done. Was she there, even? In the woods? Helping someone hide the baby and then arranging for me to find it?

It doesn't make sense.

Nancy looks down at her hands for a long minute. "You know, I don't want you to think that I don't believe you. I have to ask these questions."

"It's okay." I just want to get out of here. "Is the baby going to be okay?"

"I think so. It seems to be a healthy, full-term infant. I don't think it could have been out there for long."

I don't mean to prolong the conversation, but I have to ask. "Why would someone do this? Leave a baby like that?"

She sighs. "It happens more often than you'd think. There was a girl last year who left hers in the food court washroom at the mall."

"I think I heard about that."

"They never figured out whose baby it was. At least it was alive." For the first time, a hint of emotion, of anger, creeps into her voice. "Often they're not. Often they're killed or just hidden and left to die somewhere. Dumpster babies."

I swallow. If I hadn't agreed to go to the lake…

"Cameron, if you have any idea about who the mother could be, she urgently needs medical attention."

"Like, psychological help you mean? Counseling?"

"That, yes, but physical too. Post-partum care."

Ugh. I don't want details, so I just shake my head. "I really don't know."

She sighs. "We probably won't ever know. In these cases, most often the mothers are never identified."

"Won't someone notice? I mean, if I knew someone who was pregnant and then they weren't pregnant anymore, I think I'd notice."

"You'd think. But often these women—or girls, because they're often young—manage to hide the pregnancy completely."

I shake my head. I don't want to argue with Nancy, but I've seen pregnant women, and they usually look like they've swallowed a basketball. I can't imagine someone hiding that.

She hands me her card. "Sorry about grilling you."

"It's your job, I guess." I stick the card in my pocket.

"If you need to talk, call me."

"Why would I?"

She smiles at me, looking more relaxed now that she's apparently switched her view of me from potential Baby-Dumping Creep to Good Samaritan. "It must have been pretty traumatic, finding a newborn in the woods."

I shrug. Everything's considered *traumatic* by social-work types. "Not really," I say. "Just, you know, kind of freaky."

"Sometimes things catch up with us later," she says. "Anyway, you have my number."

Chapter Six

By the time I repeat everything to the police and answer all the same questions again, it's well past seven, and I still haven't called home. The police officer takes me out to the lake, and I show her where I found the baby.

She stands there, hands on her hips, boots planted on the trail, gazing into the darkening woods. Rain is still falling, and the trail feels soft and squishy under my feet. "So what exactly were you doing here? I mean, of all the places you could have picked to ride your bike, why did you come here?" she asks.

It's a fair question. It's not really a bike trail—in fact, there's a sign that says no bikes and no horses. And it's hardly the kind of day most people would choose to hang out at the lake. "I don't know," I say. "We used to…" I'm about to say that we used to come here as kids, but I suddenly think of Katie and instinctively decide to leave her out of it.

"We?" she prompts.

"Ah, me and some kids from school. We used to party out here in the summer. I met a girl…" I shrug. "I don't know. Some good memories here."

"Mmm. Well, it's lucky you did."

"I guess so." A bead of sweat runs down my side, and I shiver. "Can we get out of here? I'm freezing."

The cop gives me a ride back to pick up my bike, which, incredibly, is still there.

"Two miracles in one day. You really are a lucky guy," she says.

I guess that's one way to look at it.

When Mom sees me getting dropped off by a police cruiser, she freaks and demands to know what I've done *now*. As if I'm always getting brought home by the cops. She just assumes I've done something wrong. Which is an assumption I'm getting a little tired of.

"Mom, would you just listen?" I yell, exasperated. "I haven't done anything, okay? I'm not in any kind of trouble."

She stops, mid-rant, and sinks down on the couch. "Sorry, Cameron. I got your note, and when you didn't come home, I thought you'd had an accident. I've been beside myself."

Now that she's not yelling at me, I can see how stressed she looks—sort of pale and tight about the mouth. She's a major-league worrier, even when everything is going well. If it was up to her, Katie and I would wear helmets 24-7 and never leave the house.

"Sorry," I say. "I should have called. My cell phone died."

She ignores my excuse. "Yes, you should've. I was just about to phone the hospital."

"Actually, I was at the hospital." I hesitate, but there's no reason not to tell her, and besides, it'll probably be in the paper tomorrow. "I was riding my bike out at the lake and I found a baby."

She stares at me blankly. "What do you mean, you found a baby?"

At that moment, Katie appears from down the hall. She stands behind Mom, her eyes locked on mine, her face pale.

"I went out to the lake," I say. "I was riding my bike. And I found a baby. And I took it to the hospital. And now, if you don't mind, I'm going to eat something and take a hot shower, because I'm cold and I'm starving."

Mom's mouth is opening and shutting, goldfish style. I'm about to head to the kitchen to scavenge for leftovers, when Katie speaks.

"The baby...is it okay?"

I meet her eyes. "Yeah," I say. "She'll be fine."

Then I walk away. I know Mom has about a million questions, but I don't have much else to say. I just need to be alone.

I take a plate of pasta up to my room and inhale it in about thirty seconds. Then I head to the shower. I gradually turn up the water temperature until it's as hot as it can be without actually scalding me. I stand there, leaning on the wall while the spray drums against my back. I have goose bumps all over and I'm shivering. I always have a hard time warming up once I get really cold, but I think it's more that that. Much as I hate to admit it, I think Nancy was right, and I'm a bit freaked out by the whole finding-a-baby thing.

I take a deep breath and try to think.

Try to make some kind of *sense* of all this.

Katie's phone call, the baby, all those questions. What I'm most freaked-out by is the part that I didn't tell Nancy or the police officer about. What role did Katie play in this? I picture her face in the living room when she asked me if the baby was okay, but there are no clues there.

Was she—could she have been—asking me if *her* baby was okay?

I can't imagine Katie dumping a baby in the woods.

The worst thing, the thing I can't even let myself think about, is that if this baby was Katie's, then she has been pregnant for nine whole months and hiding it. She's gone through all this without any of us knowing. Without Mom knowing. Without me knowing. Which means I have let her down again.

I step out of the shower and rub myself dry, wrap the towel around my waist. My skin is boiled-lobster red, and the bathroom is totally steamed up, but somewhere deep inside me the chill is creeping back, hard and cold as glacier ice.

Chapter Seven

I detour through the living room and play a quick round of twenty questions with Mom. Same questions, more or less, though she seems to accept my discovery as a coincidence more readily than the social worker or the police officer. I retreat to my room and look up abandoned babies online. A minute later there's a knock on my bedroom door.

"Cameron?"

I close the laptop quickly. "Mom?" God, please not more questions.

"Cameron, hon? I forgot to tell you. Someone called for you earlier." She lowers her voice like it's a big secret. "A girl!"

I wish she didn't have to make it sound like a first. "Yeah? Who?"

"Audrey, she said. Such an old-fashioned name. Is she at your school? You've never mentioned her before."

"I have to do a socials project with her. Mr. McKluskey put us in pairs." And I'm forever in his debt.

"Oh." She sounds mildly disappointed. "Well, she said to call if you got in before ten."

I look at the time. Nine thirty. "Okay. I'll call her."

Audrey answers the phone on the first ring. "Hello?"

"Audrey? It's me." I blush. I doubt she's been sitting there waiting for my call. "Cameron, I mean. Um, you called earlier."

"Yeah. About getting together to work on our project for McKluskey's class."

"Right." Audrey has the tiniest bit of an Irish accent, even though she's been here since she was a kid. She has a voice I could listen to all day. It's pretty low for a girl, and really quiet. Whenever she talks in class, everyone goes silent and listens hard, because she's not a girl that talks a lot. If she talks, it's because she has something to say, and usually it's something that no one else has quite thought of. She has this sort of off-center way of looking at the world.

I clear my throat. "Um, tomorrow, maybe? After school?"

"Oh, I have band."

She plays violin. Lots of people think band is for geeks, but no one who saw her play could ever think that again. Besides, Audrey isn't the kind of girl who cares what anyone thinks. She and Dexter are well-suited that way, I guess. They're both pretty friendly to everyone.

As for me, I'd give anything to be that violin.

"Um, maybe later then? After band?" I suggest. She's probably wishing she got paired up with someone smarter. I don't know if I should invite her to come here. The thought of her being in my bedroom is a bit freaky, but I'm not working at the kitchen table with Mom offering us cheese and crackers and listening to every word we say.

"That'd be good," she agrees. "You want to meet at the library or something?"

Not my bedroom then. I wonder how Dexter feels about his girlfriend being paired up with me. McKluskey stuck him with Robert James, this obnoxious guy who is always punching everyone in the arm and laughing like a maniac. *Hee haw, hee haw, snort, snort.*

"The library is fine with me," I say. "Um, you name the time."

"Five?"

"Sure." There is nothing else we need to talk about, but the thought of hanging up depresses me. I don't feel like being alone with my thoughts. "Want to grab something to eat with me before we start work?" I ask quickly. "We could meet at the sub place instead."

"Oh. Sure. Okay."

She sounds surprised. I guess she's just thinking of this as a project. Not a chance to hang out. *Duh, Cameron, you idiot. What did you expect?*

"Well, whatever," I say quickly. "I don't care either way."

There's a brief silence. "A sub is fine," Audrey says at last. Her voice is soft, careful. "Cam? Is everything okay?"

Maybe I need to talk about it. And maybe I'm just seeing a way to keep her on the phone for a few more minutes. I don't know. All I know is that for whatever reason, I start blurting out what happened. "Ahh…I had a weird night, Audrey. I was out at the lake, you know, past the picnic area?"

"Uh-huh."

"And, um…I heard some crying. So I looked around and I couldn't see anyone. And then I saw something sticking out from behind a tree. And I found, I found…" I can't think of any way to say it that sounds anything but bizarre and melodramatic.

"God. Tell me you didn't find a dead body."

"No." I wonder if she's even going to believe me. "I found a baby."

"Jesus," she says.

"Yeah. I know. It was kind of intense."

"A baby."

49

"Yeah." Talking about it is bringing it all back—that moment of pulling back the blanket and seeing that tiny blood-smeared head. It's a video clip replaying in my mind. No, not a video. A series of stills.

Freeze frame. The woods. Muddy, leaf-strewn ground. Flash of blue. My hands are slick with sweat, and I wipe them, one at a time, against my jeans.

"Jesus. What did you do? Was it… was it alive?" Audrey's voice is even softer and lower than usual, and her accent seems stronger. She says "jaysus" instead of jesus.

"Yeah." I tell her how I bundled the baby in my jacket and rode my bike and hitched to the hospital and got grilled by the social worker and the cops. The whole story. Well—not quite the whole story, I guess. Not the part about Katie.

Chapter Eight

When Katie and I were younger, we were pretty close. I guess most twins are. We fought sometimes, over stupid stuff: who got the larger scoop of ice cream, who had more room on the back seat of the car, whose turn it was to use the computer. She usually won. Katie's always been a big girl—tall and broad-shouldered and big-boned—and I've always been a bit on the scrawny side. Mostly, though, we were best friends. Even after the boys and the girls drifted into separate groups and we stopped playing together at school, we still hung out together at home. She'd sneak into my room after Mom was in bed, and we'd play Monopoly and eat snacks we'd pilfered from the kitchen cupboards.

I don't know exactly when all that changed, but I know why. I just got tired of Katie always being so perfect. I got tired of the swimming medals in the fancy display case that Mom bought, tired of her bringing home report cards filled with As while I struggled not to drop below a C average. Most of all, I got tired of Mom going on about how proud she was of Katie. *Katie's so bright*, she'd tell everyone. I always felt like there was an unspoken second sentence: *Too bad Cameron's so much like his dad*.

I don't blame Katie for being Mom's favorite, or for being so smart. I just stopped wanting to hang out with her so much.

It's hard to be around someone who never does anything wrong.

After Audrey and I get off the phone, I lie on my bedroom floor and think about what to do. I know I should talk to Katie. The obvious thing to do is to just go and ask her what's up and why she was so desperate for me to go out to the lake. I could just ask her if she knew about the baby and whose baby it is. I don't know why I'm putting it off.

Or maybe I do.

As long as I don't talk to her, I can pretend that all this has nothing to do with her. That finding the baby was just a weird fluke. A coincidence.

The thing is, even though I'm trying not to think about it, I remember all these little things that have happened over the past few months. Things that didn't mean much to me at the time but now, post-baby, are taking on an ugly kind of significance.

Like Katie quitting the swim club four months ago. Swim club was her life.

Like the way she's been living in baggy sweatshirts all winter and spending so much time alone in her room. Not going out with her friends as much. Pretending she needs to study. Since when has Katie ever needed to study?

And Mom—who never criticizes Katie—suggesting that if she wasn't going to swim, perhaps she'd like a gym membership. *You look like you might have put on a few pounds, honey.*

Of course, a baby is more than a few pounds, right? Still…

I have to talk to her. I drag myself down the hall to her room and knock lightly.

"Yeah?"

"It's me." I push the door open and step inside. Katie's sitting up in bed in her flannel pajamas, the blankets pulled up and a book balanced on her knees. Her dark hair is pulled back in a ponytail, and her brown eyes meet mine calmly. She looks the same as always, and for a second I feel a flood of relief. There's just no way she could have had a baby. There's no way she could have hidden an entire nine-month pregnancy.

"What's up?" she asks, all casual.

"That's what I wanted to ask you," I say. "What was up with sending me out to the lake? What was up with me finding a goddamn baby there?"

She frowns. "What are you talking about?"

Christ. "Um, the baby? Remember? The one I found in the woods?"

"Yeah. That sure was lucky."

"It wasn't luck, Katie. You told me to go, remember?" I imitate her voice.

55

"Just do this one thing for me, Cameron. Just this one little thing." I stare at her. "So what was that about?"

She looks at me blankly for a few seconds. Then she just reaches out to her bedside table and turns out her light. Her voice reaches me through the darkness. "I don't know what you're talking about. And if you don't mind, I have to go to sleep."

"Katie," I say, exasperated.

She doesn't answer. I stand there in the dark for a minute, and then I turn and let myself out.

What the hell? Has she really flipped out? Or am I the one who is going crazy?

Chapter Nine

I leave early for school the next day, mostly because I don't want to see Katie. I go for a long bike ride first, hoping the rhythm of pedaling and the sound of the wind will calm me down, maybe even help me to figure it out. But it doesn't. My thoughts just take me around in circles, and I don't know what to do.

I mean, if I'm right—if this baby is really Katie's—no one is going to be happy about me digging up the truth. Probably it would be best to just forget about it.

The trouble is, finding a baby in the woods isn't the kind of thing you can just forget.

Audrey spots me in the hallway before the first bell goes.

"Cameron!" She grabs my arm. "Did you see the paper this morning?"

I shake my head. "What's it say? Was there an article about the baby?"

"Yeah." She hesitates.

I look around, glance down the hall. No one seems to be staring at me. "It didn't name me, did it? I didn't talk to any reporters or anything."

"No. It just said a teenage boy on a bike ride."

"Well, good." Audrey still seems to be looking at me kind of funny. "What is it?" I ask. "Do I have bike grease on my face or something?"

"No." She gives a little laugh.

You know how in books sometimes a laugh is described as musical? I never knew what that meant until I met Audrey. Her laugh kills me.

"What then?" I say.

"Um…it's just, in the article? It said that you went there, to the lake, because you met a girl there in the summer."

My ears and neck and cheeks are instantly red. "Oh. They put that in the paper?"

"Yeah. They quoted the police officer. It was all about what a miracle it was that the baby was found alive."

"Oh," I say again.

There's a long silence. Finally Audrey sighs. "I was just wondering…

this is going to sound really egotistical…
but I just wondered if…"

"Yeah, I meant you." She looks totally
uncomfortable. I don't want her to start
telling me about how she has a boyfriend
and all that, as if I didn't already know.
"Look, it's not really a big thing. I needed
to tell the cops something, and that was
the first thing that came to mind."

"Oh. You mean it wasn't true then?
That wasn't really why you were there?"

"Not really," I say.

She looks down at the ground for a
minute, and I wonder what she's feeling.
Confused, embarrassed, disappointed,
relieved?

"So why were you really there?" she
asks.

My heart starts racing. I want to talk
about this with someone. No. I need to
talk about this with someone. "The thing
is…I might know whose baby it is,"
I tell her.

Her eyes open wide.

"Promise me you won't tell anyone," I say.

"I won't," she says.

"I mean, really promise. Because this could really…"

"Cam. I swear I won't say a word to anyone," she says.

And so I tell her the whole story. The bell rings halfway through, but neither of us moves. When I'm done, she just makes a thoughtful little humming noise, and then she is quiet for a moment.

I force a laugh. "Yeah. Sorry. You probably think I'm crazy, huh? I mean, it sounds crazy. No one could hide being pregnant, not from people they see every day."

"No. I'm glad you told me, Cam. And people do hide being pregnant. Remember that story last year, about the girl having the baby at the mall? Leaving it in the washroom? It was all over the papers."

I nod. Next year, people would be talking about the girl who left the baby in the woods, and only I would know whose baby it was.

Audrey tilts her head to one side and frowns. "Anyway, why would Katie pretend she didn't tell you to go there if she had nothing to do with it?"

"Yeah."

"Yeah." She smiles at me and shakes her head. "So now what are you going to do?"

"Do?" I ask.

"About the baby."

"About the baby?" I sound like an idiot. An echo. A parrot. I'm feeling extremely weird. I should probably not be near Audrey while I'm in this state of mind.

"Yeah. Are you going to visit her? See how she's doing?"

It hadn't occurred to me. "Um, you think I could? It's not like I'm family or anything."

"Sure you are," she says. "If you're right—if that baby is Katie's, she's your niece. She's your mom's grand-daughter."

That hadn't occurred to me either.

"I'd go with you," Audrey says. "You know, if you want company."

I want her company, for sure. Whether I want it enough to go back to the hospital is another question. "I don't know. I guess I could call the social worker and find out if we can," I say. "I don't want to make her more suspicious though."

"I think it's natural that the person who found the baby would be curious."

I nod. "Maybe. I mean, I'd like to at least know that the baby is doing okay."

"Call then," she says. She looks like she's about to say more, but then she shakes her head.

"What?" I ask.

"What you told the cops…about meeting a girl there…"

"Yeah?"

"If that really did mean something to you…our conversation out at the lake… how come you never called me?" She tilts her head to one side. "How come you just cut me dead when I saw you at school in September?"

"I didn't."

She shrugs. "Seemed like it to me."

It had never crossed my mind that she'd want me to call. If I'd avoided her, it was just in self-defense. I don't much like rejection. "You could have called me," I say. "Anyway, you started going out with Dexter."

"Whatever," she says. "I guess we better get to class."

"Yeah." I watch her walk away. Then I yell after her. "Hey! Are we still on for after school?"

She pivots on one foot and flashes me a smile. "We are, Cameron. Because

I believe in giving people a second chance."

I spend the whole morning wondering exactly what she meant by that.

Chapter Ten

I'm heading outside at lunchtime when I see Katie. She's standing by the steps with Nikki and Luba, and she gives me a casual wave. Normally I'd wave back and walk on by, but today I stop and join them. Just like last night, I'm struck by how totally normal Katie looks. She's wearing jeans and a bright red fleece jacket, and she's laughing at something one of her friends has said. I feel a flood of relief. Not Katie. God, my brain is like a freaking yo-yo. Katie, not Katie. I eye Nikki and Luba and wonder if there is any possible way that Katie could be covering for either of them.

"How's it going?" I ask.

Katie looks at her friends and then back at me. "Fine."

Nikki grins at me. "What's up, Cameron? How was your weekend?"

"Uh, Katie didn't tell you?" If Katie had nothing to do with this baby, there's just no way she wouldn't be gossiping about this.

"Tell us what?" Luba tucks her short reddish curls behind her ears and sticks her hands into her coat pockets.

I speak slowly, trying to watch all three of their faces for any flicker of emotion. Searching for any trace of fear or guilt. "Katie didn't tell you what I found?"

Katie's face is ghost white. Even her lips are pale. She gives a tiny shake of her head. A plea.

An admission.

I grab Katie's arm. "We need to talk."

"Jeez, Cameron. What's your problem?" Luba sounds annoyed.

I don't answer. I pull Katie away from her friends. "If you don't want me to say anything, then come with me," I say. "Now. I want to know what's going on."

Katie follows me over to the side of the building and leans against the brick wall. "I'm sorry, Cameron."

"Sorry? Christ, Katie. Just tell me, okay?"

"You know already."

"Was it…are you covering up for someone else? Or…"

She shakes her head. "There's no one else."

There is a long silence. I can see all the usual people milling around, but I feel like they're all far away. Even the sound of their chatter suddenly seems muffled. It's like there's a thick glass dome over the two of us, and everyone else is outside it. I wonder if it will always feel like this, as long as we have this secret.

"You can't tell anyone," Katie says.

I still can't quite believe it. "That was your baby," I say bluntly. "You...you gave birth to that baby."

She stares at the ground and doesn't answer.

I know, but I need to hear it from her. "Katie. I'm right, aren't I?"

She doesn't look up, but she gives the tiniest nod.

"How?" I ask. "I mean, how could you do that? Leave it there?" It doesn't make sense to me that she would have picked the woods out by the lake. Not after all those trips there with Brian the Pervert. Then again, in a twisted kind of way, maybe it does. Maybe, for Katie, the woods are a place for terrible secrets.

She starts to cry softly, silent tears tracing lines down her cheeks.

"How could you have hidden it from us that you were, you know... pregnant?"

"It wasn't all that hard," she whispers. "I didn't even know I was until right at the end."

That makes no sense at all. I mean, you don't get a period for nine months and your belly gets all big and there's a baby kicking you from inside? Hello? And it's not like Katie is some dumb kid who doesn't know the facts of life.

After the enormous lie of a hidden pregnancy and an abandoned baby, this lie shouldn't seem like a big deal, but for some reason it gets right under my skin. I keep seeing that tiny baby lying there alone in the woods. Maybe I should be more sympathetic, but what I feel is fury. I want to grab Katie and shake her, slap her face, make her wake up to what she has done.

"You're sick," I tell her. "The baby could have died."

"I knew you'd find it."

Another wave of fury, this time so intense I can barely speak. "What if I hadn't been home? What if I'd said no? Did you even have a plan B?"

She just shakes her head. Her expression is closed and stubborn.

I stare at her. It's like she's suddenly become a complete stranger.

"What now?" I say. "Back to life as usual then? Pretend this never happened? Was that the plan?"

"There was no plan," she whispers. "I didn't plan any of this."

"Who...I mean, you didn't have a boyfriend or anything. So..."

"Just some guy," she says. "It doesn't matter."

My heart skips a beat and a picture of Brian the Pervert slides into my mind. If something else had happened to Katie, that might explain why she'd do something so crazy. "Were you raped?" I whisper. "Was that what happened?"

She shakes her head. "No. Just some guy at a party. I just wanted to get the whole virginity thing over with, you know? It wasn't important."

I'm not sure whether that makes me feel better or worse. Not that I would have wanted anything bad to happen to Katie, but I wanted her to have an excuse. Something to make this all less awful, less her fault. As it is, she's only one bike ride away from being a murderer. "Well, maybe it wouldn't have been important if it had occurred to you to use birth control," I say. My voice comes out cold and razor-edged.

"As it is, though, I'd say it turned out to be pretty damn important."

"You hate me," she says. "You think I'm…a terrible person, don't you?"

I shrug. There's nothing I can say, because basically she's right. That's pretty much what I was thinking.

"I couldn't tell Mom," she says. "I just couldn't."

"Mom's all right," I say. "I mean, I'm not saying she'd have been thrilled that you got pregnant, but she'd have coped. It's not like she'd have kicked you out or anything."

Katie shakes her head. "You don't understand."

"You're right," I say. "I really don't."

And then Katie just walks away. Right out of the schoolyard and off down the street. I think about running after her, but I don't do it. I just watch her leave.

Chapter Eleven

After school, Audrey meets me at my locker.

"I decided to skip band," she says.

"Oh. Okay. So…" I can see Dexter walking down the hall toward us. "Um, I think your boyfriend is looking for you."

Audrey turns and holds her arms up. Dexter grabs her and lifts her up like she weighs nothing at all, and Audrey leans her head on his shoulder and whispers something to him. He nods, his face serious, and I feel a flash of anxiety. For the first time, it occurs to me that I am probably some kind of an accessory to a crime or something. I wonder how much trouble I'd be in if this secret got out. Nothing compared to Katie, I suppose.

Dexter sets Audrey down beside me. "Okay. Call me later." He grins at me. "Lucky dog. You know who I have to do my socials project with?"

I nod. "Yeah. Robert James. Hee haw, snort." I punch his arm, Robert-style. "Sorry about your luck."

He laughs. "He's a goof. But he's okay, you know. I mean, annoying, but not a bad guy."

Dexter is too good to be true.

Then again, that's what I thought about Katie. Miss Perfect.

Audrey has her bike too, so we ride over to the downtown library and lock our bikes to the racks by the entrance. I don't want to piss her off, but I keep picturing her whispering to Dexter. Audrey's not one to gossip, but let's face it, even a saint would be tempted to repeat this story. I fumble with my lock, bang my knuckles against the bike chain, smearing grease across them. I swear under my breath. "Audrey…I know you said you wouldn't say anything to anyone, but…"

"Including Dexter," she says.

She read my mind. I grin at her. "Okay. Okay."

"But Cam…" Her forehead wrinkles, fair eyebrows drawing together. "We have to talk about it."

"What?"

"This baby…"

"Yeah."

"Have you talked to Katie? Do you know for sure it was hers?"

I hesitate for a minute, then nod. "She admitted it."

"Shit."

I don't think Audrey usually swears. The word doesn't even sound right coming from her mouth. "I know," I say. "Honestly, I didn't really think she would. I mean, I was sort of hoping she'd tell me that it was just a coincidence. Or at the absolute worst, it was a friend's baby, and she helped hide it."

"So. Now you know. What are you going to do?"

I shrug. "Well, what can I do? I mean, the baby's okay. I don't want to get Katie in trouble. I guess the best thing to do is just leave it alone, you know? Just…just let it all blow over."

Audrey pulls her jacket around her more tightly. "You can't do that."

"Watch me," I say. "Anyway, don't we have some work to do? Or do you need something to eat first?"

"Not hungry," she says.

I push the heavy door open, and we walk into the library. There are some tables on the second floor that are a pretty good space to work. No one's ever there.

I sit down, thunk my backpack onto the table and start pulling out papers from socials class. "So…"

Audrey sits down across from me, but she looks distracted. She doesn't get her notes out. She just sits there, chewing on her lower lip and staring at me.

"What?" I ask at last. "Are you still thinking about Katie?"

"It's just…well, don't you think the baby has a right to know who her mother is?"

I stare back at her. "The baby is, like, a day old. She doesn't care who her mother is."

Audrey blows out an exasperated sigh. "She'll grow up, Cam. And she will care."

"You don't know that."

"Believe me," she says quietly. "I do know that."

I feel like I'm supposed to understand, but I don't know what she's talking about. I keep picturing that tiny baby. I figure she's better off not knowing that her mother dumped her brand-new self in the woods. "I guess she'll be adopted," I say. "I mean, that's best, right? Someone who wants a baby gets to have one, and Katie doesn't get dragged through the muck."

Audrey doesn't say anything for a few seconds. She has her hands spread out on the table in front of her. Short nails, no polish, long slender fingers. Her hands are tanned much darker than her face, and she's wearing a silver ring on her finger.

"Is that from Dexter?" I ask.

She looks up at me. "What?"

"Your ring. Did Dexter give it to you?"

"No." She touches it with her other hand, twists it around her finger. "My mother. It was her mother's engagement ring."

"It's nice," I say lamely. I'm glad it isn't Dexter's ring though. Audrey doesn't seem the type to advertise that she belongs to someone.

"My adoptive mother," Audrey says.

The words hang in the air for a moment before I make the connection. "You're adopted?"

She nods.

I'm fumbling backward through our conversation, connecting the dots. "Is that what you meant? When you said you knew that the baby would want to know who its mother was?"

She nods again. "I mean, my mom and dad are awesome. They're totally my parents in every way, and I wouldn't change that. But there's still this missing piece, you know? This question."

"Have you, you know, tried to find your…?" I fumble for the right words, and Audrey interrupts me.

"Birth parents? No. I probably will though. Mom says she'll help me."

"Huh. But what if…I mean, if your mother, I mean birth mother, had done something like this…abandoned you somewhere…you'd hardly want to meet her, would you?"

"I would."

"Seriously? Man." I picture the baby again—how completely helpless it was, just lying there in those blankets, wailing. "I think I'd be too pissed off."

She shrugs. "Well, I'm not saying I want to hang out with my birth mom, necessarily. But even if she doesn't want to meet me, I want to know more about her. I mean, I'm her kid, at least in the biological sense. I have a right to know who she is and what she looks like and why she gave me up for adoption.

And I think this baby you found…well, I guess I just think she has that right too."

Audrey's eyes are shining a little too brightly, but I don't say anything. Because even if she's right, I don't see what I can do about it.

Chapter Twelve

By six o'clock, we've managed to rough out an outline for our presentation, but Audrey's pretty subdued. I figure she's still thinking about the baby.

"So." I slide my binder and some loose pages of notes back into my backpack.

"So?"

"I guess I'll see you at school tomorrow." I hold my breath for a second.

"Unless you still want to go get a sub or something?"

"I should get home," she says.

"You're pissed at me, huh?" I may not get the best grades, but when it comes to figuring out what people think, I'm not a complete idiot.

"Not pissed, exactly. I just think…well. I guess I have a hard time believing that you're really not going to do anything."

I look at her. "Audrey, come on. What can I do? Call the cops? Rat her out?" I shake my head. "She's got enough problems without getting charged."

"Maybe she wouldn't be," she says. "I mean, she told you to go there. She made sure that the baby was found."

"Yeah." That's the part that surprises me most, to be honest. I mean, she hid the whole pregnancy, gave birth alone, and then—when she'd basically got away with it all—she blew her cover to save the baby. Not to make out like she's some kind of hero—I mean, she still left a baby in the woods. But it gives me some hope that she's not totally…cold. Messed-up, but not messed-up enough to let the baby die.

"It was pretty lucky, me finding the baby," I say. "I might not have. Could have missed it just as easy. If it had stopped crying a few minutes earlier…" I wonder what Katie would have done if I'd come home and said nothing. I don't think I ever want to know the answer.

Audrey picks up her bike helmet and fiddles with the chin strap. "You know, I don't think you're doing your sister any favors by keeping this a secret."

I raise my eyebrows.

"I think you should tell someone. That social worker, maybe."

I don't think she's really thinking about Katie at all. "Maybe you're kind of identifying with the baby, you know? Being adopted and all that."

"So?" she says.

Her eyes flash. I should see the danger signs and back off, but I don't. "So maybe you're putting the baby's interests ahead of Katie's."

"Maybe I am. I get that you found the baby, and I get that Katie's your sister. But do you really think you know what's best for either of them? Because if you do, you're kidding yourself."

"I know I have to protect Katie."

"Protect her? You think you're protecting her?" Audrey raises her voice, and a few people look our way curiously. "Katie is seriously lost, Cameron."

"Shh," I say. "Keep your voice down."

Audrey just glares at me. "You know what? She's not going to get any help if you keep her little secret." She swings her pack over her shoulder and stands up, her bike helmet dangling from her wrist. "You're choosing to be a part of something really twisted, Cameron.

So don't pretend you can't do anything. You're making choices here. You're that baby's uncle, okay? If you just walk away, you're abandoning her too. You're just as lost as Katie."

"At least I abandoned her at a hospital."

Audrey just shakes her head. "I have to go, Cam. Think about it, okay?"

Mom and Katie are just sitting down to eat when I get home.

"Chicken stir-fry," Mom says. "You hungry?"

I sit down across from Katie and dish myself a bowlful without meeting her eyes. "Starving."

"That's my boy. When are you ever not hungry?" She slides a loaf of bread my way.

I glance up at her and force a grin. Mom's pretty young—not quite forty—

Robin Stevenson

and she looks even younger. No gray hair, no wrinkles except a few tiny lines around her eyes. She doesn't look old enough to be a grandmother, and I wonder what she'd do if she knew she was one. She's always been gaga about babies. I wonder if she'd want to be a part of this baby's life, even if Katie doesn't want anything to do with it.

"You okay?" she asks. "You look like you're miles away."

"Yeah, sorry. Just thinking about school," I say. "This assignment I have to do."

She frowns. "Tell me you haven't left it until the last minute."

"I haven't," I say, stung.

"Good. Because some people can get away with procrastinating, but not you. Katie, now—she's always done well under pressure."

I sneak a glance at Katie across the table. I wonder if she's noticed that Mom's doing it again. She hates it too—she says it's embarrassing, that it makes her feel like a big fake. Tonight, though, she doesn't even seem to be listening. I guess she's got bigger things on her mind. She hasn't touched the food, and I can't help noticing that she's awfully pale.

"Excuse me." Katie pushes her chair back and stands up, balancing herself with one hand on the table.

Mom frowns. "You okay, hon?"

"Yeah, yeah. Just…you know." She gestures to the washroom and heads off down the hall.

Mom waits until the door closes. "Cameron, is something going on with your sister?"

Christ. "I don't know. Why? What's up?"

"She came home early and said she didn't feel well." Mom's forehead furrows. "I wonder if something happened at school."

"Not as far as I know," I say.

I listen to Mom talking about Katie for a while. Katie and the swim team, Katie's university options, whether Katie is better suited for law or medicine. How well Katie handles pressure.

I wonder how Mom would react if she knew what Katie had done when she was *really* under pressure.

Mom looks at Katie's untouched plate. "This isn't like her. I hope she isn't coming down with something."

I stand up. "I'll go check on her."

Katie's in the bathroom. I knock softly on the door. "It's just me."

"Go away." She sounds like she's crying.

"Are you okay?"

The toilet flushes. "Just leave me alone, Cameron."

A sudden unease prickles at the back of my neck. I test the door handle, expecting it to be locked, but the door swings open. "Sorry," I say, embarrassed. I'm about to close it again, but then I glimpse Katie. She's not on the toilet. She's sitting on the edge of the tub, in her T-shirt and underwear. Her jeans are balled up in a heap on the floor, and there's a thin line of bright red blood running down the inside of her leg.

Chapter Thirteen

Katie grabs a towel and covers herself with it.

"Do you mind?" She glares at me defiantly.

Okay, obviously I'm invading her privacy, but…"Katie? Are you…you know, bleeding?" Duh. There's blood smeared on the floor and the toilet seat, and the tiny garbage can is full of blood-stained pads.

She doesn't say anything, but her face is awfully white.

"You need to see a doctor," I say. "We should go to the hospital."

"I can't."

"Katie…"

She starts crying. "Cameron, you can't tell anyone. You promised."

Did I? I can't remember promising anything. Anyway…"This is serious, Katie. You need to see a doctor."

"I'll be fine."

Talk about denial. "You're not fine, Katie. You're…look at you." There's a big lump in my throat. "Come on. We'll go to the hospital. I'll go with you. We can tell Mom you're not feeling well. We don't have to say anything about, you know…"

"Since when do we go to the hospital because we're not feeling well? As if she'll just accept that." Katie rubs the back of her hand across her eyes and wipes her nose on her sleeve. "Anyway, the doctors...I don't want anyone to find out."

I'm way out of my depth here. "Look, I'm not just going to let you bleed to death."

My words hang in the air, too loud, too harsh. I didn't even mean it—didn't really think she was in danger of dying—but now that I've said it, it suddenly feels like a possibility. Like this might really be life or death.

"I'd rather die than have everyone know," Katie whispers.

I don't believe her. I don't believe she really wants to die. Still, if she can pretend she's not pregnant for nine months, maybe she can pretend she's not in any danger now. And maybe I'm wrong, and she really would rather die than be found out. "Stay there," I say. "I'll be right back."

In my room, I quickly dial Audrey's number. I need a reality check. I need to talk to someone who's not in total denial. Ring. Ring. Ring. No answer. I hang up, frustrated, and stare at the phone for a minute.

"Cameron!"

I stick my head out into the hall. "Mom? I'm just making a call."

I can hear her banging dishes into the dishwasher, and I figure I've got about a minute before she comes down the hall to see where Katie and I have disappeared to. I take a deep breath and rummage through the pile of papers on my desk until I find the card that the social worker gave me. I quickly dial her number.

"Hi, you've reached Nancy, emergency room social worker for…"

Recorded message. I hang up. Crap, crap, crap. I grab a clean pair of sweats from Katie's room and head back down the hall to the washroom. My heart is banging away, my palms sweating, my stomach in knots. I knock on the bathroom door.

"Go away," Katie says.

I turn the handle. She's locked it. "Katie. Let me in."

There's no answer.

"Katie. If you don't let me in, right now, I'm calling an ambulance." I wait a couple of seconds. "I mean it."

There's a silence, a pause. Then the door opens. Katie's paler than ever, her freckles standing out like grains of pepper against her white skin, her forehead and upper lip beaded with sweat. "I don't feel good," she says.

"I'm taking you to the hospital," I say.

"What about Mom? What are you going to tell her?"

I haven't thought this through. "That you're sick?"

She starts crying again, and I get this glimmer of how she must feel—this sense of her world falling apart, of all the pieces crashing down around her. My chest feels tight. "Katie," I say, "it's all going to be okay." I don't believe this, but I say it anyway.

Grandma Bess, Dad's mother, used to have this embroidered picture on her wall that said *This Too Shall Pass*. I always thought it was a depressing saying, but it comes to mind now—like maybe if we can just hang on, if Katie can just get through this, that there might be life somewhere on the other side.

"I can't do this," she says.

"You don't have a choice."

She leans against the wall.

"Let's go," I say. I open the bathroom door and hold out my hand to her. "Right now, or I really will call an ambulance."

To my surprise, she takes my hand and follows me willingly, and I wonder if, somewhere deep down, she is relieved to have someone else making the decisions.

"There you are," Mom says. She sounds irritated. "Were you planning on coming back to actually eat your dinner, Katie?"

"Mom, Katie's sick," I say. "I'm going to take her to the hospital."

Mom puts down the dishtowel and one hand flies up to her mouth, fingertips pressed against her lower lip. "What's wrong?"

I look at Katie. She doesn't say anything. "I don't exactly know," I say. It's only half a lie.

"I'm bleeding," Katie says. Her voice is a whisper.

Mom looks at her. "God. You look awful, Katie."

"Can I take your car?" I say.

Mom stares at me. "If Katie really needs to go to the hospital, I'll take her. But Katie...is it just a bad period? Why don't you go lie down for a while? I'll bring you a heating pad."

I shake my head. "Mom, she needs to go to the hospital. Seriously. Can I take the car?"

She gives me a strange look. "Is this some weird twin thing? Like when you were six and you got lost and Katie knew where you were?"

"Something like that," I say. I don't even remember that incident, but if it helps...

Mom shrugs, torn between irritation and worry. "Fine, then. I'll come too."

Mom drives. No one talks much in the car. Fortunately, the hospital isn't that far, because the silence is pretty uncomfortable. Also, Katie looks like hell. She's in the backseat, and I keep twisting around to look at her, but she won't meet my eyes. Mom seems annoyed, like we're totally overreacting, but I'm not going to be the one to tell her the truth. I figure that's Katie's decision to make.

When we get to the hospital, Mom and Katie go up to the reception desk. I hang back, clench my hands into fists and try to breathe evenly. I hadn't quite realized how scared I was, but as soon as we walked into the emergency room, I felt the weight of my fear start to lift a little. It's a huge relief to know that no matter what kind of mess this ends up in, at least Katie will be taken care of. At least she won't bleed to death alone in our bathroom.

The emergency room is pretty quiet: a couple of old men sitting reading magazines, a skinny haggard-looking guy pacing back and forth restlessly, a dark-haired woman with a toddler whimpering in her arms. The last time I was here, I was holding Katie's baby in my arms.

I can't believe that was only last night.

Chapter Fourteen

After a few minutes, Mom comes and sits down beside me. Katie goes to the washroom. When she comes back, she picks up a battered copy of *People* magazine and pretends to read it.

Mom crosses her legs and sighs. "I'm sure that nurse thought we were overreacting. Honestly. I bet we'll be here for hours."

I sneak a sideways glance at Katie. She doesn't look up. She hasn't told them a thing. I've relaxed too soon: she won't bleed to death at home alone, but apparently she's quite prepared to bleed to death right here in the emergency room. "I'll be back in a minute," I say. I walk in the direction of the washrooms, but I don't stop there. I head right past them, down the hallway to Nancy's office. The door is closed, so I knock, and to my surprise, she answers.

"I'm just on the phone with someone. Can I…" She breaks off and steps into the hall. "Cameron, right?"

"Yeah. Good memory."

She just waits, eyebrows slightly raised, face calm and serious.

"My sister's in emergency," I say. "Can you…can you make sure someone sees her soon? She's…she's bleeding."

"Ohh." She nods, blinks, nods again. "You'd better come in." She tells whoever is on the phone that she'll call them back. Then she turns to face me. "Your sister... that was her baby you brought in?"

"Yes. I didn't..." I was going to explain that I hadn't known that at the time, but it no longer matters. "She's bleeding. A lot. I got her to come in, but... well, our mom's here too."

Her face is carefully expressionless. "Your mom doesn't know."

It doesn't sound like a question, but I answer it anyway. "Katie doesn't want her to find out."

Nancy shakes her head. Then she picks up the phone. "Margo? It's Nancy. Is there a teenage girl there with her mother? Yeah...No, I don't think that's all it is...Yeah, I know...Remember that baby that was brought in last night? Yeah...No, the mother doesn't know. Can you get her seen fast? I think she might be having a postpartum hemorrhage."

When Nancy gets off the phone, she turns to me. "You know, Katie isn't going to be able to keep this a secret."

I'd figured that much out. "So what's going to happen?"

"First thing is to get your sister taken care of," she says. "Then we'll go from there."

"Will you call the police?"

She shakes her head. "Not my job. Child welfare is already involved, of course—the baby will be placed in a temporary foster home. She doesn't need to be in hospital; she can go as soon as arrangements are made. Now, though…" She shrugs. "Well, I'll let them know about your sister. They'll want to talk to her."

"And they'll call the police?"

"Cameron…" Nancy looks at me seriously. "They might have to. I don't know exactly what will happen. But no matter what, you did the only thing you could do."

I hope she's right.

"Do you want to go back to the emergency room? Katie probably is being seen by a doctor, but you could go sit with your mom…"

I shake my head. "I don't want to be the one to tell her, and it's too weird, with her not knowing. She was trying to get Katie to take a Midol and lie down, and I was freaking out thinking she might die."

"You can stay here for a few minutes, if you want," she says. "I'm going to go see how things are going with your sister."

When Nancy's gone, I pull out my cell phone and call Audrey again. This time she picks up.

"Audrey? It's me. Cameron."

"Hey, Cameron. What's up?" She sounds surprised to hear from me.

"I'm at the hospital. I just wanted…" I don't know what I want to tell her, or what I want her to do. I'm not even sure why I called her.

"Are you okay?" She drops her voice to a whisper. "Is the baby okay?"

I suppress a flicker of irritation. "The baby is fine. It's Katie."

"Oh…Jeez. What happened?"

"She's pretty sick, I guess. Mom's here too, but she still doesn't know." I swallow a lump in my throat. "It's going to be a huge mess."

"Oh. Wow. That's…" She trails off.

"Are you alone? Or is someone else there with you?"

"Um, Dexter's here. He's playing some game online. You know…wizards and dragons and all that. I'm not that into it. I was just reading."

Dexter's there. Of course he is. I can't help feeling disappointed though. I don't know what I expected—that she'd come rushing to the hospital and somehow, magically, help me get through this. I mean, I know she has a boyfriend. I know we're just friends, and barely even that.

"I guess I better let you go," I say.

"Cameron, do you need…do you want us to come? Dexter has his car here— we could be there in ten minutes."

I almost laugh. "Nah. Thanks. But, you know…I don't really want anyone else to know about this."

I can hear her smacking her forehead. "Duh. Sorry. Of course you don't." There's a brief pause. "Cam? Do you want me to come? 'Cause I know Dex would let me borrow his car, no questions asked."

I really want to hate that guy, but I just can't do it. "Nah. That's okay. I just wanted to tell you."

"You sure?"

"Yeah, I'm sure. I'll call you later." I hang up, feeling better already. She's willing to leave her perfect boyfriend to come hang out at a hospital with me. Not that I'm reading too much into that, but I'm pretty sure it means we're at least friends. That she gave me a second chance, and I haven't blown it yet. And who knows. Maybe she'll get tired of having a perfect boyfriend.

I know how hard it can be to be around someone who is always perfect. I'm thinking that maybe perfect is over-rated, and for the first time I wonder what it has been like for Katie, always having to be the perfect one. I wonder what it will be like for me and her, after we get through all this. I wonder whether things will ever go back to the way they were. I wonder whether we'll want them to.

Chapter Fifteen

There's a knock, and the door slowly swings open. I half stand up, wondering if Nancy has seen Katie.

Nancy steps through the door. Mom is right behind her.

I sink back into the chair. I look from one of them to the other, wondering what has happened, what has been said, what Mom knows. Wondering how much trouble I'm in. Then an awful thought flashes into my mind. "Katie?" I say. My voice comes out as a croak. "Is she okay?"

Nancy nods quickly. "She's getting excellent care, and the doctor says she should be just fine."

"Oh. Good. Then…" I look at Mom. Her face is pale and strained, nose swollen, eyes puffy and pink-rimmed, her usual mascara washed off. "I guess you talked to Katie."

Nancy answers for her. "The doctor met with your mother and Katie together. Katie told your mom about her pregnancy."

"And…"

She nods. "And about the baby."

I look at Mom. "I'm sorry."

"Me too," she says. She starts to cry again. "How could I not have known? My own daughter…under my roof! I don't understand this."

Nancy leads Mom to a chair, and she collapses into it. Nancy slides a box of tissues across the table toward her. "It's a big shock," she says.

Well, duh.

Mom looks at me. "Thank God you found the baby."

"Katie made sure I did," I say. As I say it, I realize that's what I will tell anyone who asks. There's no need for anyone to ever know how easily it could have ended differently. I guess now that's all I can do to protect Katie. I hope it is enough.

"You mustn't blame yourself," Nancy tells my mom. "This happens more often than you would think."

"Katie says she didn't even know she was pregnant," Mom tells me.

I nod. "I know. She told me that too. But I don't really get how that's possible."

"It's called dissociation," Nancy says. "She may have sometimes suspected it, but the idea was so frightening—so unacceptable—that she pushed it right out of her consciousness." She opens a drawer of her filing cabinet and rifles through some papers. "I've got some information for you about it that you might want to look at later. But basically, she is telling you the truth. She really didn't know."

"And then, when she realized she was…she was in labor…" Mom wipes her eyes with a tissue.

"She panicked," Nancy says. "She drove to a place she could be alone, she delivered the baby…"

"And left it in the woods," Mom says flatly. She starts crying again.

"And told me," I say quickly.

Mom nods and sniffs. "Thank God." She looks at me, then at Nancy. "It's so hard to believe this. Katie's never been in trouble at all, she's a straight-A student, an athlete…"

"Yeah, she's pretty much perfect," I say. I try not to sound bitter, but it's a bit much, after everything that has happened, to have to listen to Mom listing Katie's achievements.

"I can see how that might make it hard for her to admit to herself that she was pregnant," Nancy says. "You know, often these girls are high achievers. They're kids who don't want to disappoint their parents, who are afraid of rejection."

"That's ridiculous," Mom says quickly. Too quickly. "I'd never reject my kids. Never."

"Of course not," Nancy says. "But subconsciously, maybe she didn't want to let you down."

There's a long silence. I don't know what Mom is thinking, but what Nancy is saying makes sense to me. If you are already seen as a bit of a screw-up, what's one more problem? But if your whole life is constructed around being perfect…

well, I can see how an unplanned pregnancy would mess that up.

I watch the second hand ticking on the large white clock above Nancy's desk and I think about the baby that is at the center of all this. Even though I held her and everything, she doesn't seem quite real to me—not like an actual person—but, of course, she is. I think about Audrey and her questions about her own birth mother. A missing piece, she had said. I know she's right. This baby does have a right to know, someday, about all of this. Katie's baby, my niece, Mom's granddaughter.

"Can I see the baby?" I ask Nancy. For some reason, I'm blinking back tears myself. "Just, you know, to know she's okay?"

Mom looks startled. "I'd like to see her too. Can we?"

Nancy nods. "I'll take you up to the neonatal unit. Come on."

The baby is even smaller than I remembered. Nancy picks her up, and I lift up my arms, but she hands her to Mom instead.

Mom holds her a little stiffly, away from her body, and looks down at the little face. It's a bit squashed-looking, sort of puffy, with creases around her eyes. Not exactly cute.

"She looks just like you did," Mom says. "Just like you."

Huh. I take a closer look. "She's tiny."

Nancy laughs. "She's almost eight pounds. Nothing tiny about her."

Mom touches the baby's cheek with her fingertips. "So soft." Her eyes are suddenly teary again. "If Katie changes her mind…if she wanted to keep the baby…would there be any chance of that?"

Nancy perches on the edge of a long table. "I honestly can't say. That would be for a judge to decide." She sighs. "If she'd abandoned the baby at a hospital or handed it to someone instead of leaving it where she did, the situation would be very different."

"She made sure I'd find her," I say quickly. "You know that."

She nods. "That would be in her favor, for sure."

We are all quiet for a long moment, all of us looking at the baby. Mom hands her to me, and I hold her against my chest and remember riding my bike with her tucked inside my jacket, listening to her breathing and praying she would live. "Good luck, little baby," I say.

I'm pretty sure Katie won't change her mind, but before we leave, I snap a quick photo with my cell phone. Maybe it'll help Katie to know that the baby really is okay.

Chapter Sixteen

Mom and I sit in the emergency room together. We don't talk much. Every so often Mom shakes her head and says she still can't believe this, or wonders aloud what will happen. At one point she gets up and leaves a message for a friend who is a lawyer.

"She'll call back," Mom says. "She'll know what we should do."

I nod, relieved. She's going to do her best to protect Katie too. "I didn't know how you'd react to this."

"I don't know how to react," she says. "Katie…well, I've always worried about her."

I raise my eyebrows. "Come on. She's always been perfect. I'm the one who screws up."

"No." Mom shakes her head. "You've had your challenges at school, but you've always been yourself. Katie doesn't have that confidence. She's always needed to be perfect." She looks at me. "I tried to tell her she was, but maybe that wasn't the best way to handle it."

I squirm in my seat and look across the room at a couple of little kids who are tussling over a picturebook. "I don't know," I say. "I always thought she really was."

Mom gives a sad laugh. "Goddamn Brian," she says. "If I'd handled that differently, maybe this wouldn't have happened."

I catch my breath. We never talk about Brian.

"I don't think I'll ever forgive myself," she says. "For not protecting you two."

"I'm fine," I protest. "Nothing happened to me."

"It could have though."

"Well, it didn't."

I look up and meet her gaze for a second, but her eyes are so full of sadness that I have to look away. "Mom…"

"It's okay. I'm okay." She reaches out and puts her hand on my knee. "Thanks for taking care of your sister, Cameron."

"Mom." I don't know how to say this. "Katie's going to have to live with what she did, you know? I mean, forever. She's going to have to live with this forever."

"I know." She closes her eyes for a second. "God, I know."

"So…well, you'll help her, right? Make sure she gets counseling and all that. And…you know. Help her deal with this."

"Of course I will." She squeezes my knee. "Cameron? There is nothing I wouldn't do to help either of you. I just wish Katie had known that."

Eventually a nurse comes out and tells us that Katie has been moved up to a medical ward and that they want her to stay overnight. "She's fine," she tells us. "Stable. We just want to keep an eye on her."

"Can I go see her?" I ask. I turn to Mom. "By myself, just for a minute?"

She nods and squeezes my shoulder. "I'll wait outside."

Katie looks pale, but otherwise not too bad. She's lying down with her head and shoulders propped up by three fat pillows. "Cameron."

"Hey, Katie." I wonder if she's mad at me—if somehow she thinks it's my fault that she's here and everyone knows. "Look," I say. "I'm sorry I couldn't keep your secret. I was so scared that, you know…"

She interrupts. "It's okay. It's sort of a relief, in a weird way. Like now the worst has happened. It's been hanging over me for so long, this dread…I think this is almost easier."

I swallow. "Yeah. I told them that you made sure I found her, anyway."

"And she's okay, right? The baby?"

"I just saw her." I pull out my cell phone. "Do you want to see a picture?"

Katie hesitates; then she shakes her head. "I don't think so. Not now, anyway." She pulls her bottom lip between her teeth. "You know how I said I didn't know I was pregnant?"

I nod.

"Well, sometimes I think I sort of suspected. Just for a minute, here and there. But I wouldn't let myself think about it, you know?" She sighs. "I guess you and Mom must think I'm crazy."

I shake my head. "Nah. Well. Yeah, maybe a little."

She gives me the tiniest hint of a smile. "Yeah."

"Are you...you think you might change your mind? And want to see the baby?" I don't know why, exactly, but I want her to say yes.

She doesn't though. She just looks at me for a long moment and says nothing at all.

"I guess not," I say lamely. "It's just...I don't know. I thought you might, I guess."

She shrugs. "I don't suppose they'd let me anyway."

"They might."

"Maybe." Katie closes her eyes. "I think I have to sleep a bit."

"Mom will want to see you," I say. "I'll get her, okay?"

She nods and I leave the room. I'm thinking about what she said—about how the worst is over. I hope she's right. I hope she'll talk to the counselors and figure out how all this happened and find a way to get through what lies ahead. I hope she'll put this all behind her and go back to being Miss Perfect again. Swim club and university scholarships and all that. I wouldn't mind.

I find Mom and tell her that Katie wants to see her. Then I find a chair in the hallway, and I sit there and wait.

It's weird to think that even if Katie can eventually put this all behind her, there is a whole new person—all eight pounds—just upstairs, whose life is just beginning.

More than anything, I hope her life is a good one. I don't know if it's possible, but I'd sort of like to be a part of it. Not a big part. Something though—even if it's just sending a birthday card once a year. I'd just like to know that she's doing okay.

I guess, in a way, finding her makes me feel sort of responsible for her. And like Audrey said, she's my niece. No matter what Katie decides to do.

Robin Stevenson is the author of a number of novels for teens, including *Big Guy*, *Inferno*, *A Thousand Shades of Blue* and *Out of Order*. She lives in Victoria, British Columbia. More information about Robin and her books is available on her website at www.robinstevenson.com.

For more information on all the books in the Orca Soundings series, please visit www.orcabook.com.

It's a bundle of blankets. I pull back the top layer cautiously, and there it is. It's a baby.

WHEN CAMERON RESCUES A BABY ABANDONED in the woods, everyone says it is a miracle. A stroke of luck that he just happened to be there, riding his bike along that trail, and heard the baby's cry. But Cameron has a secret: it wasn't just luck. He was there because his twin sister Katie begged him to go. Did Katie know about the baby? Is she covering for someone? At first Cameron just wants some answers...but once he knows the truth, he has to decide what to do with it.

orca soundings

$9.95
RL 3.2

ISBN 978-1-55469-200-2

ORCA BOOK PUBLISHERS
www.orcabook.com

9 781554 692002